I Don't Know What to Call My Cat

Written by Simon Philip   Illustrated by Ella Bailey

Houghton Mifflin Harcourt

Boston   New York

I have a new cat.

She turned up on my doorstep one day,
looking hungry.

She obviously liked the dinner I gave her,
because she's stayed ever since.

That's fine.
I like cats.
There's just one tiny problem.
I DON'T KNOW WHAT TO CALL MY CAT.

I thought Kitty would be just right.

It wasn't.

Then I tried Princess High-and-Mighty.

But she didn't seem to like the dress.

I tried out more.

PAT

Lorraine

TRICIA

ETHEL

tracey

JANE

Betty

They're all good names . . .

. . . but not for a boy.

I tried hard to think of a name for a boy cat.

Butch.
Rambo.

Arnie.
Rocky.

None of them were right.

Then I tried Mr. Maestro.

My cat seemed to like it too . . .

. . . until I joined in.

Where had he gone?

I looked and looked.

But I couldn't find him anywhere.

Fresh

Not even at the zoo!

So I gave up.
There was nowhere else to look.
Maybe he would have stayed
if I'd thought of the right name.

I missed my cat . . .

. . . but the pet that followed me home from the zoo cheered me up.

And it turns out Steve was really easy to name.
Never mind that he was a bit moody.

Our days out together were lots of fun,
even when Steve was a little naughty.

Yet I did sometimes have the feeling we were being watched.

Everything went perfectly until the day we had unexpected visitors. One of them looked a little familiar.

I'm not sure why Steve had to leave so quickly.

But the good news is . . .

. . . my cat came back!
He had a new collar—
and a name!

Well, I guess that fits. He *was* very tricky to name.

And maybe one pet at a time is best for everyone.